The Great Pumpkin Switch

story *by* **MEGAN McDONALD**

pictures *by* **TED LEWIN**

Orchard Books   New York

For Aunt Do
and Uncle Jim, the original
"Old Flypaper"
　　　—M. McD.

For John Frank and
in memory of Betty Frank,
and for Tony Cosentino/Grandpa
　　　—T.L.

Orchard Books, 95 Madison Avenue, New York, NY 10016

Manufactured in the United States of America.
Book design by Mina Greenstein. The text of this book
is set in 16 point ITC Bookman Light. The illustrations
are watercolor paintings.
Hardcover　10　9　8　7　6　5　4
Paperback　10　9　8　7　6　5　4　3

Library of Congress Cataloging-in-Publication Data
McDonald, Megan.
The great pumpkin switch / story by Megan McDonald :
pictures by Ted Lewin.　p.　cm.
"A Richard Jackson book"—Half t.p.
Summary: An old man tells his grandchildren how he and
a friend accidentally smashed the pumpkin his sister was
growing and had to find a replacement.
ISBN 0-531-05450-0 (tr.)　ISBN 0-531-08600-3 (lib. bdg.)
ISBN 0-531-07065-4 (pbk.)
[1. Pumpkin—Fiction.　2. Brothers and sisters—Fiction.]
I. Lewin, Ted, ill.　II. Title.
PZ7.M478419Gr　1992　[E]—dc20　91-39660

Sit close now, and I'll tell you.

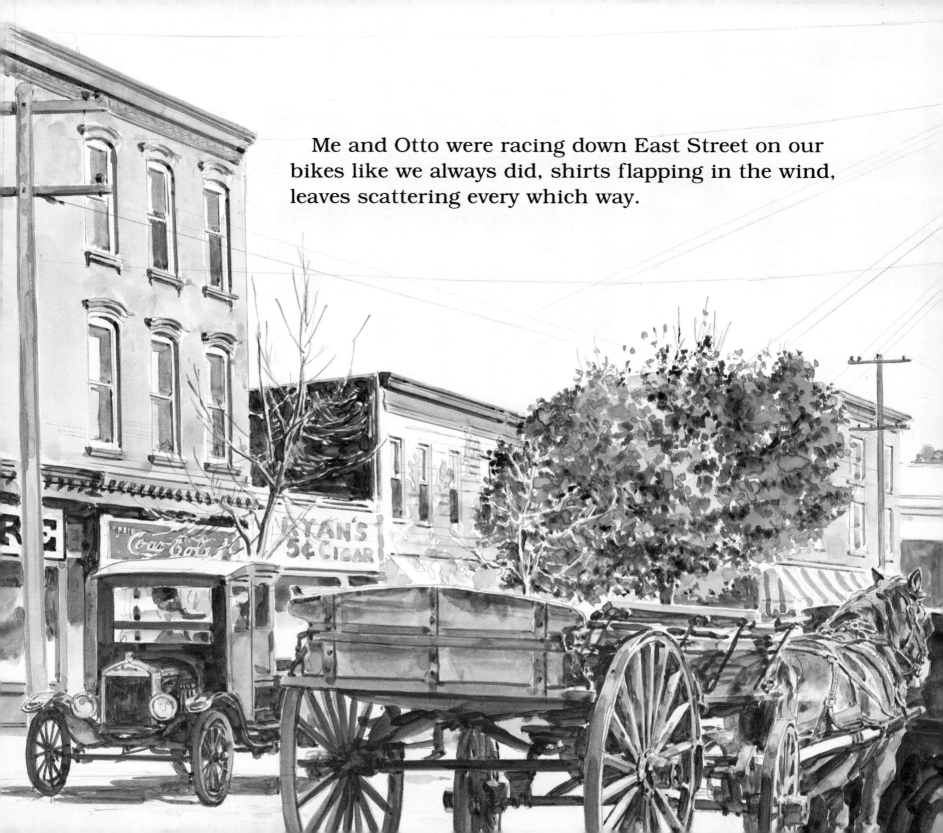

Me and Otto were racing down East Street on our bikes like we always did, shirts flapping in the wind, leaves scattering every which way.

We dumped our bikes in my backyard.

"Hey, Otto, it's apple butter day today. Help me stir the stuff before Mama hollers."

I lifted up the big wooden paddle. Stirred it round and round and round in that sweet-smelling soupy brown murk until our heads were spinning. Bees buzzed all around us.

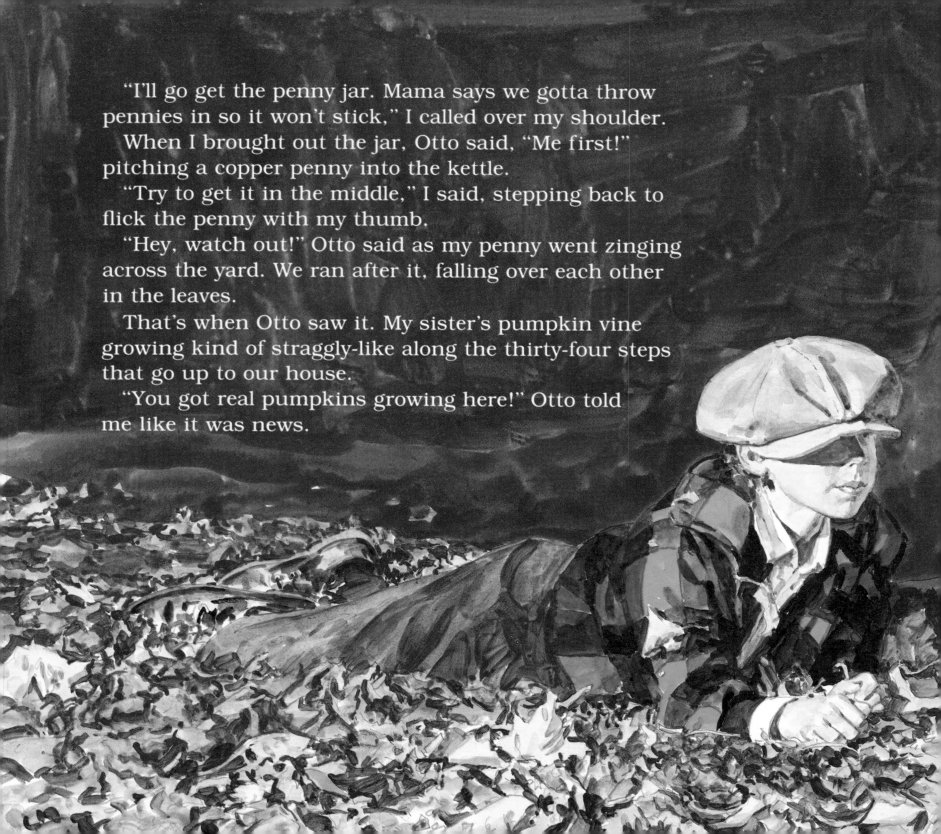

"I'll go get the penny jar. Mama says we gotta throw pennies in so it won't stick," I called over my shoulder.

When I brought out the jar, Otto said, "Me first!" pitching a copper penny into the kettle.

"Try to get it in the middle," I said, stepping back to flick the penny with my thumb.

"Hey, watch out!" Otto said as my penny went zinging across the yard. We ran after it, falling over each other in the leaves.

That's when Otto saw it. My sister's pumpkin vine growing kind of straggly-like along the thirty-four steps that go up to our house.

"You got real pumpkins growing here!" Otto told me like it was news.

"Yeah, Rosie's trying to grow the biggest pumpkin ever. Bigger than a bushel basket, she says! For the Sunflower Girls."

"The *Sunflower* Girls?" Otto scrunched his cap up like it was a bonnet.

"I know, I know."

Just then we heard the *clippety-clop* of horses' hooves on the stones. "Abba-no-potata-man!"

"Hey, it's the Potato Man. I'll race ya."

"Remember when you used to be scared of old Mr. Angelo?" Otto asked.

"Was not."

"Were too."

Rosie came running out of the house and down the steps, pigtails and ribbons flying in the air.

"Mr. Angelo! Mr. Angelo! See my pumpkin? I growed it all by myself." Rosie pointed to her prize pumpkin.

"Did ya, now? She's a beaut! Will you trade her for a bag of oranges?"

" 'Course not. I'm not tradin' Big Max for any old oranges. My brother would probably just squeeze 'em in my hair. I'm trying to get Sunflower Girls' patches for my quilt. I saw about it in a seed catalog."

"Told ya." I nudged Otto. "And your pumpkin's gonna be as big as a bushel basket, right, Rosie?"

"Bigger!" Rosie stretched her arms wide.

"That I gotta see," said Mr. Angelo. "Now I better finish my rounds, and you boys better go on inside. You too, Rosie. Storm's comin'." The Potato Man's wagon was off trotting down East Street quicker than you could say "cabbage patch."

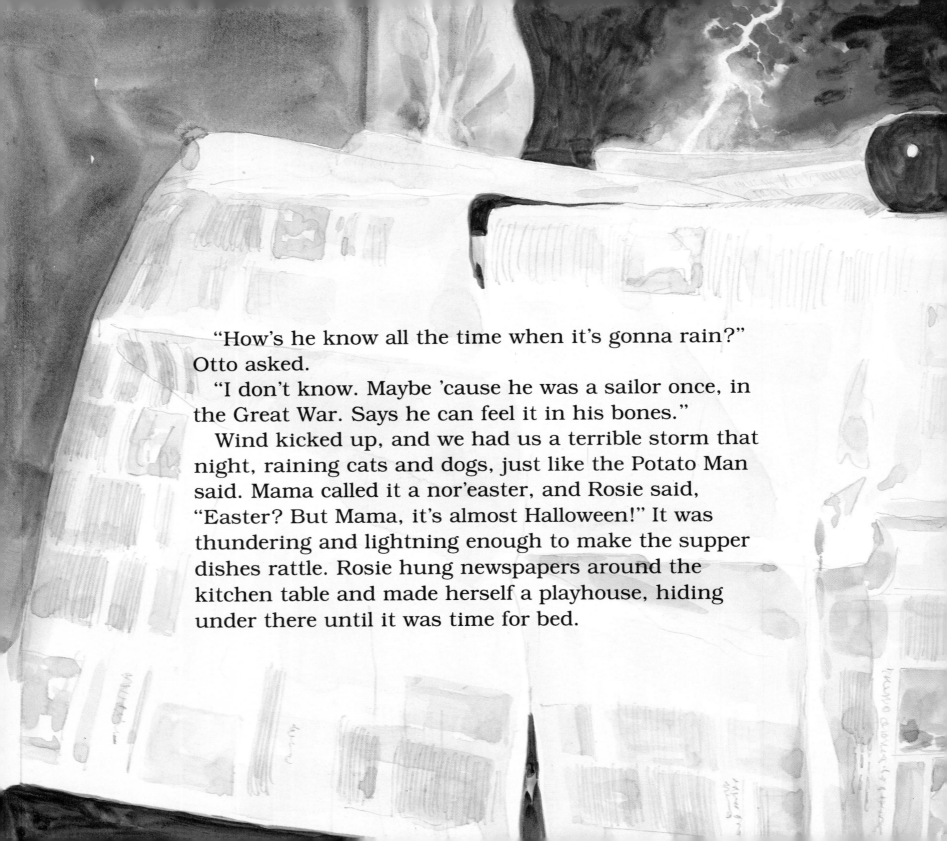

"How's he know all the time when it's gonna rain?"
Otto asked.

"I don't know. Maybe 'cause he was a sailor once, in
the Great War. Says he can feel it in his bones."

Wind kicked up, and we had us a terrible storm that
night, raining cats and dogs, just like the Potato Man
said. Mama called it a nor'easter, and Rosie said,
"Easter? But Mama, it's almost Halloween!" It was
thundering and lightning enough to make the supper
dishes rattle. Rosie hung newspapers around the
kitchen table and made herself a playhouse, hiding
under there until it was time for bed.

Middle of the night, my dog Dukie woke me up with his howling. Chocolate chip cookies were the only thing would quiet him down. Then I heard a *crrr-rrrack!* loud as Fourth of July fireworks. Mama said, "Back to bed!" but next morning our old poplar had fallen right across the front walk.

In sooner than no time, Mama had me out clearing away branches. After piano lessons, Otto came over, asked, "Why don'tcha use a saw?"

"Not allowed."

"But your mama didn't say anything about *me* not using a saw."

I ran like greased lightning around back to the toolshed, Otto right behind me, and climbed up on a barrel of soap chips to reach the saw.

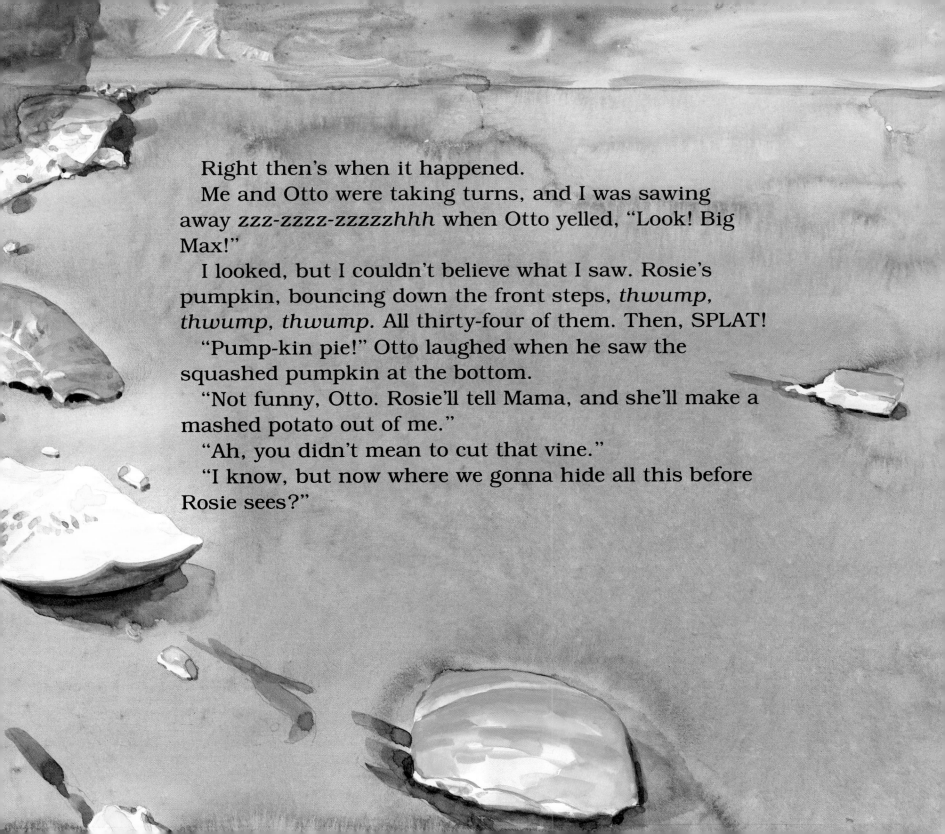

Right then's when it happened.

Me and Otto were taking turns, and I was sawing away *zzz-zzzz-zzzzzhhh* when Otto yelled, "Look! Big Max!"

I looked, but I couldn't believe what I saw. Rosie's pumpkin, bouncing down the front steps, *thwump, thwump, thwump.* All thirty-four of them. Then, SPLAT!

"Pump-kin pie!" Otto laughed when he saw the squashed pumpkin at the bottom.

"Not funny, Otto. Rosie'll tell Mama, and she'll make a mashed potato out of me."

"Ah, you didn't mean to cut that vine."

"I know, but now where we gonna hide all this before Rosie sees?"

"How about Mrs. Hadley's pig next door? That pig would eat the dirty socks right off your feet."

"Here. Carry some in your shirt. Let's go!"

That pig squealed and snorted when we tossed the pieces over the fence, seeds and all.

"We could get another pumpkin before Rosie finds out, whaddya think?"

"The Potato Man!" we both said at the same time.

"Abba-no-potata-man!"

We found him down on Diploma Street. When I told him about Rosie's pumpkin, his shoulders shook laughing. "Tell you what. This here pumpkin's the biggest I got."

"It looks just like Rosie's Big Max!"

"Thing is, it'll cost you boys twenty cents."

"We got twenty cents, Mr. Angelo," I told him.

"We do?" Otto was looking at me like I just sprouted horns.

"Sure. You'll see. Can we give you the money later?"

"I think I can trust you boys until then." The Potato Man winked his good eye. "Now, let's see if you can lift this thing without making squash."

Took me and Otto both to load the Potato Man's pumpkin into my Radio Flyer wagon. "This thing must weigh fifty pounds," Otto was saying.

"Biggest pumpkin I ever did see. Hey, thanks, Mr. Angelo," I called over my shoulder.

Soon as we got home, Otto and me tied that pumpkin on the vine good as ever.

"Rosie'll never know," I told Otto.

"Hide the string under a leaf," he told me.

We barely got the saw back in the shed before Rosie came skipping down the steps. She let out a scream I'm sure they could have heard all the way down the river in Aliquippa, and went running into the house.

"She knows," I told Otto.

"You'll just have to tell her. Here she comes."

Rosie was pulling Mama's arm. "Look, Mama. Look! Look how much Big Max grew!"

"Look at that. Would you look at that," Mama was saying like she believed it. "Must have been all that rain. Right, boys?"

"Yeah, Rosie," I told her. "That rain grew your pumpkin bigger than a bushel basket."

"Big as a washtub!" Rosie laughed, spreading both arms as wide as she could reach and spinning herself in circles until she was dizzy. "Now I can get all the patches I need for my Sunflower Girls' quilt, Mama!"

"C'mon inside now, and we'll have some of that apple butter the boys worked so hard on."

"Mama, you know how all those pennies stick to the bottom?" I asked.

"Yes?"

"And you know how much you hate scrubbing out that kettle?"

"Yes!"

"If me and Otto scrub out that kettle real good, can we keep some of those pennies?"

"We'll see," Mama answered. "Right now it's time for—"

"Apple butter!"

"And hot chocolate?" Rosie asked.

Mama nodded. "And hot chocolate."

"Don't stop now, Grampa."

"Yeah, Grampa, did that pig really eat dirty socks?"

Grampa leaned back, shaking his head to himself. "I don't know, but Mama always did make us wear clean socks."

"Did you get the pennies, Grampa? To pay the Potato Man?"

"Me and Otto paid Mr. Angelo his twenty cents the very next day. Pennies came out of that apple butter all bright and shiny as new. I even kept one for a lucky penny. Carried it in my pocket for the longest time."

"Do you still have it, Grampa?"

"Can we see it, Grampa?"

"That's for another time. Another story."